Favorite Fairy Tales

Adapted for the LeapPad by Stephanie Shaw
Illustrated by Niall Harding

Table of Contents

I. Beauty and the Beast

Once upon a time, there was a rich **merchant** who had three daughters. The two oldest were pretty but were selfish and mean. The youngest was kind and good-hearted. She was also so pretty that she was known simply as "Beauty." Her sisters were very **jealous** of her.

The older sisters loved to spend money on fancy clothes and jewelry. They were always going to dances. Beauty was smart and **curious**— she liked to read a good book or spend time with her father.

The merchant owned **cargo** on a ship that was lost at sea. With the loss of this ship and other troubles, the merchant was left very poor. The only thing he still had was a small house in the country. With tears in his eyes, he told his daughters they all must now go there and work for their living.

They moved to the country, and Beauty worked hard cooking and cleaning for her father and sisters. Beauty always tried to be cheerful and make the best of things, unlike her sisters, who were lazy and angry.

One day their father got a letter telling him that the cargo ship lost at sea had arrived in **port**. He told his daughters they might not be so poor after all!

The merchant said he was going to the port to get his cargo and sell it. The two oldest daughters asked him to bring them back gifts of fancy dresses and jewelry. Beauty did not ask for anything.

"Isn't there anything I could bring you, Beauty?" asked her father.

She thought of how much it would cost her poor father to buy the gifts her sisters wanted. She said, "A rose would be nice."

When the merchant got to the port, he found his cargo had been stolen, and once again, he was left with nothing. Feeling sad, he started toward home.

On the way, it started to snow. The snow grew heavy, and the wind blew so hard that the merchant could not see his way. Soon he became lost in a forest. Night fell, and the merchant, cold and tired, could hear the **howling** of wolves nearby. Just as he was sure he would die, he saw the gates to a beautiful palace.

He put his horse in the **stable** and fed him, then knocked on the palace door. No one came, but the door swung open and he went inside. "Is anybody home?" he called as he walked through a grand hallway. He went into room after room, but he saw no one.

In one room, he found a fire in the fireplace and a delicious dinner set out on a table. He waited a long time for someone to appear, but when no one did, he sat down and ate the food himself.

After eating, he looked around some more. He found a bed that looked so cozy that he lay down and fell asleep.

The next morning he awoke to find clean clothes next to him, a cup of coffee by his bed, and some fruit to eat. He couldn't believe it!

After getting dressed and eating, he decided to walk through the garden before getting his horse and going home.

In the garden, the sun was shining and there was no snow on the ground. Trees were in bloom, and **fountains** were full of water. Just as he turned to leave, the merchant saw some roses. "Beauty wanted a rose," he said to himself as he picked one to take to her.

Suddenly a big, ugly **beast** with sharp **fangs** and **claws** stood over him. "How dare you steal my roses!" **growled** the Beast. "I gave you food and let you stay in my home. Is this how you repay me? I shall kill you for this."

"Forgive me!" **begged** the merchant. "I only wanted one rose as a gift for my youngest daughter."

"I shall **spare** your life—but only if your daughter comes here of her own free will to take your place," said the Beast. "If not, you must promise to return here yourself to die. And if you try to get away, I will find you. Now go!"

The merchant returned home carrying the rose. He cried as he told his daughters of his promise to the Beast. At once, Beauty said she would take his place at the Beast's palace. Her father said, "No, no, no! I won't have it!" They **argued** for hours. Beauty finally said, "My mind is made up. You cannot stop me from following you back to the palace, so you might as well show me the way."

Heavyhearted, the two of them set off. Beauty's two sisters **pretended** to be sad that she was leaving, but they had to rub their eyes with an onion to make themselves cry.

When Beauty and her father got to the palace, they saw no one—but a delicious meal **awaited** them in a cozy room. "There is so much food here that the Beast must be trying to make me fat before he eats me," thought Beauty.

After they ate, they heard the Beast's footsteps. Beauty shook in fear as the big, **furry** Beast came into the room. "Good evening, Beauty," he said. "Have you come of your own free will?"

"Good evening, Beast," she said. "Yes, I've come willingly."

"Then you may stay, but your father must leave first thing in the morning," said the Beast.

The next morning, Beauty and her father said good-bye to each other with tears in their eyes. Then Beauty began to look around the palace. She was surprised to find a door with the words "Beauty's Rooms" on it. Inside, she found several wonderful rooms, including a library with shelves of books and a **harpsichord**. *I won't run out of things to do,* Beauty thought. *If the Beast plans to eat me right away, surely he would not have* **bothered** *with all of this.*

That evening the Beast joined her at supper. She told him about how she had looked around the palace.

"You may do whatever you wish," said the Beast. "Everything here is yours. But, tell me, do you find me very ugly?"

After a moment, Beauty replied, "Yes, I do." Then she added, "But I think you're also very kind."

"Will you marry me?" asked the Beast. Beauty was shocked and afraid of making him angry by her reply.

"Don't be afraid," he said. "Just say 'yes' or 'no.'"

"No," said Beauty. "I won't marry you."

"Good night, then," he said, and he left the room.

They lived like this for several months. Beauty would spend her days alone—reading, playing music, or walking in the garden—and the Beast would join her for supper and talk with her. She grew to enjoy talking with him and always looked forward to seeing him.

She had good food to eat, beautiful clothes to wear, and lots of things to keep her busy. In fact, she was very happy living at the palace, and she had grown very fond of the Beast. But every evening he would ask her to marry him, and every evening she would say no.

In a magic mirror at the palace, Beauty was able to see her family. She saw her father looking sad and ill. Her sisters had married, so her father was alone, and Beauty was worried about him.

One evening the Beast said, "Even if you won't marry me, will you promise never to leave me?"

"I will—if you will let me go see my father one more time," said Beauty. "I promise to return in seven days."

"You may go," said the Beast. "But if you don't come back in seven days, my heart will break and I will die."

Beauty went home to spend a week with her father, who she found sick in bed. She told him how kind the Beast was, and that made her father feel much better.

Her sisters came to visit and were jealous of Beauty's happiness and her beautiful clothes. They **secretly** decided to try to make her break her promise to the Beast. If she stayed away for more than seven days, perhaps the Beast would get angry and eat her. They begged her to stay a few more days, and she agreed.

On the tenth night she spent at her father's house, Beauty had a dream in which she was walking through the palace garden and found the Beast dying and calling for her.

She awoke shaking and saw how strong her feelings were for the Beast. She rushed back to the palace on horseback.

She ran up the stairs calling for the Beast, but there was no reply. She looked through room after room but could not find him. Recalling her dream, she ran into the garden.

There she found him lying on the ground, his body stiff and his eyes shut as though dead.

"Oh, no!" she cried as she threw herself on him and hugged him.

"Don't die! Please don't die!" she said, her tears falling on his fur. Just then, the Beast moved a little and opened his eyes.

"You didn't come back," he said quietly. "Now I'm dying."

"I'm sorry!" Beauty cried. "You must not die! I love you, and I want to marry you!"

As she spoke, a blaze of light lit up the sky and the sound of fireworks and music filled the air. She looked up at the sky and when she turned back, the Beast had **disappeared** and in his place at her feet was a handsome young prince.

"Beast, where are you?" she cried, looking around.

"You are looking at him," said the prince. He told her how a fairy had put a terrible spell on him, turning him into a Beast until a beautiful girl agreed to marry him.

"Thank you for breaking the spell," he said. "My dearest Beauty, I shall love you forever."

Right away, a splendid wedding was planned at the palace. Beauty's father and sisters came.

But the fairy who had **enchanted** the prince put a spell on Beauty's sisters. She turned them into **statues** to stand by the palace gates until they were sorry for their wicked ways. They stand there still.

Beauty and the Beast were married and lived happily ever after.

II. City Mouse and Country Mouse

Once upon a time, there were two mice who were **cousins**. One mouse lived on a pretty farm in the country. It was far from the noisy city. She slept in a barn with cows and horses, curled into a furry ball in the straw.

When she was thirsty, she drank the fresh, clean water from the river. When she was hungry, she ate acorns that fell from oak trees in the woods. Sometimes oats slipped from the horse's **feed bin**. Then Country Mouse invited her friends to share her special treat.

"It's our lucky day! Come and eat! Yummy oats for everyone!" she cried.

One sunny day, her cousin, City Mouse, came to stay with her. He looked around.

Making a face, he shook his head. "What an ugly barn," he said. "And just look at that nest in the straw. How **quaint**." He rolled his eyes. "My house in the city has a feather bed."

"Perhaps my home is not very grand," Country Mouse agreed. "But taste the water. Isn't it fresh? Isn't it clean? Just look how it **sparkles** in the sunshine."

"Your life here is very plain, Cousin," he said. He looked sorry for Country Mouse. "My poor cousin! You have so little here."

Country Mouse looked around. She began to feel sorry for herself, too. She looked at the red barn. For the first time, she saw that the paint was **peeling**. Her cozy bed in the straw looked very . . . well, plain. She ate a few of the acorns she had gathered for their breakfast. They tasted dry now, instead of delicious.

"Your life in the city must be wonderful!" Country Mouse sighed.

"Oh, it is, it is!" City Mouse **boasted**. "Come and stay with me. It will be fun. We'll eat like kings and queens."

"All right. I will." A **vacation** in the city— how exciting!

The very next day, Country Mouse went to stay with her cousin in the big city. They rode a bus to get there.

Oh, there were so many people in the city. People were everywhere! She and City Mouse had to run this way and that to escape their feet. Trucks and cars sounded like metal monsters. Her paws and tail were soon covered with dirt. By the time they got to City Mouse's fancy brick house, Country Mouse was shaking with fear.

Her cousin ducked into a mouse hole. "Come right in!" he proudly told her. "Don't be shy. Welcome to my house."

Country Mouse was amazed. City Mouse lived in a huge house with fine sofas, chairs, and tables. There were wonderful pictures on the walls and soft carpets on the floor.

Her cousin's mouse hole was in the corner of a kitchen **pantry**, where food was kept cool. Yellow cheese filled a blue dish on one shelf. A loaf of soft white bread lay on another. There was also a cake with bright pink frosting that said "Happy Birthday, Sue." The blue candle in the middle was shaped like the number 7.

Mmm! Delicious! Country Mouse had never smelled such wonderful food.

"Help yourself," her cousin told her. "Eat as much as you like. Don't be shy. This is the big city."

"Oh, thank you," she said. "I'd love a piece of cheese."

But when she went to nibble some—ZAP! There was a loud snapping noise. Something dark **flashed** past her. Whatever it was, it almost caught her around the neck. She **squeaked** in fright and jumped back. "Oh, my! What was that?"

"A mousetrap, silly. It almost got you, too. You really should look where you're going, cousin. This isn't your old farm, after all."

He thought she was stupid. She could tell. A tear filled her eye. Didn't he care? She had almost been killed!

"Oh, well. Never mind. Have some cheese," he said.

"Thank you." At least he was trying to be nice, she thought.

Country Mouse nibbled at the cheese, just to be polite. But it was not nearly as yummy as she had expected. Her near escape from that awful trap made her mouth dry. Her poor little tail was still trembling!

"It was a long bus ride," her cousin said. "You must be tired. How about a nap?"

"A nap would be good," Country Mouse agreed.

 "Later, we'll have cake for supper," City Mouse promised. "None of those awful acorns for us city mice, eh?"

That evening, after their nap, City Mouse led the way out of his mouse hole. He ran across the dark pantry.

Country Mouse followed him.

"Some birthday cake, my dear?" He was trying to be the perfect **host**.

"Yes, please. But . . . what about traps?" Country Mouse **whispered**.

"I already checked!" her cousin said happily. "It's all clear. Don't worry. Now, go on. You first. You are my **guest**, after all. Have some birthday cake."

Country Mouse gulped. "All right." Her voice was squeaky. She was still scared.

Inch by inch, Country Mouse moved toward the cake. Just as she was about to take a tiny bite of pink frosting, she heard an awful sound. It was not the terrible ZAP! of a metal trap as it snapped shut. No. This sound was far worse. It was a sound known to mice all over the world.

It was the sound of CAT.

"MEEOOWWW!" it **yowled**.

Country Mouse froze in place. Her eyes were round with horror. Two huge green eyes **blazed** at her from the shadows!

"Hmm, perfect!" purred the cat. "A mouse. My favorite fast food! Come to kitty, little mouse!"

With a hiss, the cat jumped onto the shelf. It landed with all four paws in the birthday cake. The frosting was sticky and just like glue. The cat was stuck!

Angry, it stopped to lick the frosting from its claws.

It was their only chance.

"Run!" yelled City Mouse. "Run for your life!"

Country Mouse ran. She ran as hard and as fast as she could. She ran across the pantry. Down the mouse hole. Out of the house. Through the city streets. She did not stop until she reached the bus station and the bus that went to the country.

"But why are you leaving so soon?" her

cousin cried. He ran after her. "You must admit, we have wonderful things here in the city."

"Yes. You do," Country Mouse agreed. "But the price for your yummy yellow cheese and your frosted cake is much too high for me!"

"Price?" asked her cousin. "But the food is free!"

Country Mouse shook her head. "No, it is not. Each day, you risk your life for a piece of cheese or some cake. A life is a very high price to pay! At the farm, I have all the acorns a mouse could ever want. I only have to look on the ground."

"But . . . but . . ." began City Mouse.

Country Mouse continued. "The water I drink is fresh and sweet. My bed in the barn is not as fancy as yours is, but it is a safe place to sleep. Oh, what a lucky mouse I am! Why didn't I see it before? I have so much to be thankful for!"

With that, Country Mouse jumped onto the bus. "Good-bye, cousin. Thank you for having me."

That night she slept in her little bed in the old barn. Her friends, the horses and cows, were happy to see her back.

Asleep in her **snug** nest, Country Mouse dreamed of acorns. Yummy, sweet acorns—all she could ever want—and no traps or cats to worry about. Ever.

Oh, it was so good to be home!

III. The Emperor's New Clothes

Once upon a time, there was an **emperor** who loved to wear fancy clothes.

This emperor was very **vain** and spent most of his time in his bedroom changing his clothes. "You look marvelous," he would say to himself in the mirror. Then he would go outside and show off his newest **outfit** to the people in his castle.

One day, two **crooks** who had heard about the emperor's **vanity** came to the city where he lived. They told everyone that they were very talented weavers who could make the most beautiful cloth in the world, full of wonderful patterns and rich colors.

"Besides being beautiful, our fabric is also

invisible to anyone who is stupid or who is bad at his job," the crooks claimed.

The emperor heard about the weavers and their special cloth. *What wonderful clothes that fabric would make,* he thought. *I would be able to tell who in my* **empire** *is clever or foolish. I must have it!*

The emperor had the weavers come to his castle at once. He gave them a big bag of gold coins so that they would start working right away. They were shown a room with two **looms** and the emperor gave them fine silk and gold thread to use to make the cloth.

The crooks hid the silk and gold thread in their pockets. Then they pretended to weave on the empty looms.

Two days passed, and the emperor was very curious about how the weavers were doing. He decided to send a trusted old **minister** to check. The minister saw the two weavers pretending to work on the empty looms.

"Oh, dear," he said to himself. "I cannot see anything at all. But if I say I can't see the cloth, everyone will think I am stupid and I might lose my job."

"Come and see our beautiful cloth," said one of the crooks, waving the old man closer. "See how shiny it is. And see the delicate patterns. What do you think?"

The old minister put on his eyeglasses and said, "Why . . . it's lovely. Yes, just splendid. I'll be sure to tell the emperor how wonderful it is."

The two crooks became bolder and asked for more money and more silk and gold thread, which the emperor immediately gave them. Again, they secretly put the thread in their pockets and the looms stayed empty.

A few days later, the emperor sent another **adviser** to see the weavers. Of course, the man could not see anything. But he was afraid that people would think him stupid if he **admitted** that, so he said nice things about the cloth to the weavers. To the emperor, he said, "It's **magnificent**."

Everyone in the city was talking about the cloth. Everyone wanted to see it. Finally the emperor decided it was time for him to see it. With a group of **officials**, he went to the room where the weavers were working.

What's this? thought the emperor. *I can't*

see a thing! Am I stupid? How could this happen to me?

But to the other people in the room, the emperor said, "My, my, what **exquisite** cloth! Simply the best!"

The emperor would not—could not—admit that he saw nothing. And all the people with him looked at the looms and saw nothing as well. But they nodded and said, "Yes, your Majesty, it's amazing! You *must* have clothes made from this fabric for the big parade next week."

So the emperor gave the two weavers even more gold coins, as well as some jewels, and asked them to make him a special outfit.

The whole night before the parade, the weavers sat up and pretended to sew the new clothes. First they cut the air with a pair of scissors. Then they sewed the air with needles that had no thread in them. They burned more than sixteen candles during the night, as **proof** of how late they had stayed up working.

Early the next morning, the emperor came to try on his new clothes. The two crooked weavers raised their arms as if lifting something up and said, "Here are your pants and here is your

mantle, Your Majesty."

The emperor took off all his clothes, and the weavers pretended to put the clothes on the emperor. They even pretended to **fasten** buttons on the invisible outfit.

"This suit is as light as a spider's web, so Your Majesty will not even feel it," the crooks told the emperor.

"How wonderful you look!" everyone said. "The clothes fit you so well, and you are so handsome!"

Finally it was time for the big parade through the streets of the city. All the people who lived there were gathered along the streets or leaned out their windows to see the emperor in his new clothes.

The emperor was nervous because he could not see any clothes on his body. But he said, "I am ready."

Two **servants** bent down as if to pick up the ends of the emperor's long mantle. They, too, did not want anyone to know they could not see anything.

The emperor marched in the parade under a beautiful **canopy**. Everyone in the street clapped and admired the emperor's new clothes.

"Beautiful!" shouted one person.

"What a splendid mantle!" said another.

"Look at how well everything **matches**," noted a third person.

Everybody pretended to see the clothes since nobody wanted to appear to be stupid.

But then a small boy on the street pointed and said loudly, "Look, Father, the emperor is naked!"

There was a stunned silence.

Then all the people started to repeat the little boy's words over and over until the whole crowd shouted, "The boy is right! The emperor has no clothes!"

The emperor's face grew very red as he realized that what they were saying was true—he *was* naked.

But I must *go on with the parade,* thought the emperor, still unable to admit his own foolishness. So he lifted his chin proudly and just kept walking.

His two servants, holding the emperor's invisible mantle off the ground, looked at each other and rolled their eyes. Then they stepped forward and followed their leader.

Meanwhile, the crooks were making their way out of town, counting their money and laughing at how wonderfully their plan had worked on the foolish emperor.

IV. The Frog Prince

One day long ago, a beautiful young princess went into the woods near her father's castle. She was holding her favorite toy, a golden ball, which she liked to toss in the air.

Under an old tree stood a well full of water. The princess tossed her ball so high she could not catch it, and it fell into the well. The well was deep, and she could not even see her ball.

The princess started to cry. She cried louder and louder.

"What is wrong, Princess?" asked a little voice. "Your weeping would make a rock feel sorry for you."

Surprised, the princess looked around and saw a frog poking its ugly head out of the well water.

"I'm crying because my favorite golden ball fell into the water," she told the frog.

"Don't cry," he said. "I can get your ball. But what will you give me if I do?"

"I'll give you whatever you want—my clothes, my jewels, even my crown!" said the princess.

The frog said, "I don't want your clothes or jewels or crown. But if you promise to love me and be my friend and to let me eat off your plate, drink from your cup, and sleep in your bed, then I'll dive down and get your golden ball."

This frog is talking nonsense, thought the princess. *He thinks he can live with people when all he can do is sit in the water and* **croak**. *It doesn't matter what I promise him.*

To the frog she said, "I promise anything you want, if only you get my ball back."

When the frog heard this, he swam under the water and soon came back with the ball in his mouth. He threw it on the grass.

The princess, **overjoyed** to see her toy, picked it up and ran away. "Wait for me! Wait for me!" cried the frog. "You promised to take me with you!" But the princess **ignored** his cries and ran home without him. He went back into his well.

The next day when the princess sat down to eat with her father the king and all the **courtiers**, there came the sound of something splashing up the marble staircase. Then there was a **knock** at the door, and a voice called, "Princess, open the door for me!"

She ran and opened the door. There sat the frog. She slammed the door, came back and sat down. The king, seeing how **frightened** she was, asked, "Why are you so afraid? Is there a giant outside who wants to carry you away?"

"Not a giant," she said. "Just a **slimy** frog. My golden ball fell in the well and he got it. I promised him he could live with me here, thinking he could never get out of the well. But now he's at the door, and he wants to come in!"

At that moment there was another knock at the door, and a voice cried:

"Open the door, my princess dear,
It is your true love standing here.
Remember the promise you made to me.
Open the door and together we'll be."

The king said, "Daughter, you must keep

your promise. Go and let him in."

She opened the door, and the frog hopped inside and followed her back to her chair. There he stopped and called out, "Lift me up to sit next to you." The princess did not want to, but the king told her to do it.

Then the frog wanted to be placed on the table next to her plate so that they could eat together. She did this, but everyone could see she did not want to do it.

The frog stuffed himself, but the princess didn't feel like eating a bite. After the meal, the frog yawned and said, "I'm full, and now I'm tired. Carry me to your room so that we both may go to sleep on your pillow."

The princess started to cry. She was afraid of the cold frog and did not want to touch him. The king got angry and said, "He helped you when you were in trouble, so you cannot turn him away."

She picked up the frog with two fingers and carried him to her room. She put him on her pillow, and he went to sleep. The next morning the frog woke up, hopped out of bed, down the stairs, and out of the house. "Thank goodness he's gone," the princess said. "I shall be annoyed by him no more."

But she was mistaken. That night she once more heard a knocking on her door. When she opened it, the frog hopped in and went to sleep on her pillow.

The third night, the frog did the same thing. But when the princess awoke the next morning, she saw not an ugly frog but a handsome prince standing at the end of her bed and looking at her with kind and beautiful eyes.

He told her a wicked witch had turned him into a frog and that a princess had to let him sleep on her pillow for three nights to break the spell.

"My only wish is that you will come to my father's **kingdom** and marry me," said the prince. "I promise to love you as long as you live."

The princess agreed to marry him. Later that morning, a fine **carriage** pulled by eight white horses came to the castle door. They set out full of joy, heading for the prince's kingdom, where they lived happily ever after.

The Gingerbread Man

Once upon a time, there was a little old woman who loved to bake. She lived with her husband in a pretty, white house. Just the two of them lived there; they had no children. Inside the house was the tidy little kitchen where the old woman did all her baking.

One day she decided to bake a **gingerbread** man. She made the **dough**, rolled it out flat, then cut out the shape. She gave him a little, round body and head, two arms and two strong legs.

Then she put two **raisins** on his face for eyes, a cherry gumdrop for a nose, and red **licorice** for his mouth. She used the last of the raisins to make little buttons down the front of his jacket.

The little old woman was very pleased with her **creation**. She put him in a pan and popped him into the hot oven to bake. Then she got busy sweeping the kitchen and forgot all about the gingerbread man until a wonderful smell reached her nose.

"My gingerbread man smells as though he's almost done," she said as she opened the oven door to check on him.

"Oh, yes, he's ready," she said, looking at his deep brown color. She pulled the hot pan from the oven and put it on the table to cool. "He looks good enough to eat."

As soon as she said that, the most amazing thing happened. The little gingerbread man jumped up from the pan and hopped from the table to the floor!

"You can't eat me!" he cried as he ran toward the kitchen door. In a flash, he was out the door and across the garden.

"Stop, stop!" yelled the little old woman, running after him. Her husband, who was working in the garden, saw her chasing the **runaway** cookie, and he joined her.

As the gingerbread man jumped over the

garden fence, he shouted over his shoulder:

"Run, run, as fast as you can,

You can't catch me.

I'm the gingerbread man!"

The little fellow ran down the road **lickety-split**, leaving the little old man and the little old woman far behind.

Soon he came to a barn where some men were **threshing wheat**. The **threshers** saw him and tried to catch him. "Stop, stop," they cried. "We're hungry, and you'd make a delicious snack."

The gingerbread man waved and laughed, but he just kept moving as he shouted:

"I escaped from a little old woman,

I got away from a little old man.

Run, run, as fast as you can,

You can't catch me.

I'm the gingerbread man!"

The threshers heard his **taunt** and kept chasing him, but they couldn't run fast enough to grab him. Farther down the road, he met a big brown cow.

"Why are you moooving so fast?" she asked. "Slow down and let me munch on you. You would go nicely with a glass of milk."

"I'm not cow **chow**!" he cried, then added:
"I escaped from a little old woman,
I got away from a little old man,
I **eluded** a bunch of threshers.
Run, run, as fast as you can,
You can't catch me.
I'm the gingerbread man!"

The cow ran after him, but she was not very fast, and soon the gingerbread man had left her far behind. That's when he saw a large yellow dog.

"Stop!" barked the dog. "Stop or I'll bite those tasty little legs of yours."

"My legs are boneless—so you wouldn't like to **gnaw** on them," **teased** the gingerbread man. Then he said:

"I escaped from a little old woman,
I got away from a little old man,
I eluded a bunch of threshers,
I **foiled** a silly cow's plan,
Run, run, as fast as you can,
You can't catch me.
I'm the gingerbread man!"

Away he ran down the road, with the dog barking and chasing him. But the dog wasn't fast enough to catch him.

Then a gray horse stepped out in front of him. "**Whoa** there, little **fella**. Where's the fire?" asked the horse.

"No fire. I just don't want anyone to eat me," said the gingerbread man.

"I don't want to eat you, unless you're made of oats," said the horse. "But you're very fast, and I'd like to race you."

So the horse and the gingerbread man raced down the road. But eventually the horse stopped running and said, "You're faster than I am, little gingerbread man. Good-bye and good luck!"

Now the gingerbread man was feeling quite proud and **cocky**. "No **sirree**, nobody can catch me—not all those people, not the cow, or dog, not even the horse."

At that moment he saw a fox running toward him through a field. "Good day to you, young man," said the fox.

"Good day," said the gingerbread man who was still running. "I can't stop to talk or you'll eat me."

"Why would I want to eat you?"

"Because I'm tasty and everyone wants to

eat me," replied the gingerbread man.

"I hate to **disappoint** you, but I have no desire to eat you," said the fox. "I'm a fox, and foxes don't eat gingerbread. It **upsets** our stomachs."

By now the fox was running along next to the gingerbread man. But they had come to a wide river and had to stop. The gingerbread man knew he could not swim across—if he got himself wet, he would fall apart.

The fox **perked** up his ears. "I think I hear something. Is anyone chasing you?"

"Well, the horse gave up, but the old woman, the old man, the threshers, the cow and the dog may still be after me," he said, but he didn't hear anything.

"Oh, yes," said the sly fox. "I hear a dog barking and people shouting. Quick, you'd better jump on my tail, and I will carry you across the river."

The little gingerbread man jumped on the fox's tail, and the fox swam into the river.

When they were a little way from the shore, the fox said, "Little gingerbread man, I'm afraid you'll get wet on my tail. You'd better get on my back." So he jumped from the fox's tail to his back.

In the middle of the river, the fox said, "The water is getting deeper here, and I'm afraid you'll fall off. You'd better jump on my shoulder so you can hold on to my neck."

The little gingerbread man did as he was told and jumped on the fox's shoulder. Then, as they got near the other side of the river, the fox said, "The river runs faster here than I **expected**. Quick! Jump on my nose and I'll be able to keep you dry!"

As soon as he reached the shore, the fox threw back his head and snapped open his mouth. The gingerbread man fell in.

"Oh, dear!" he cried. "I'm **one-quarter** gone!"

That was followed by "Oh, I'm half gone!" and then, "Uh-oh, I'm **three-quarters** gone!"

At last his tiny voice could be heard from inside the fox's throat: "I'm all gone!" Then he never spoke again. It was sad, of course, but gingerbread cookies are made to be eaten!

VI. The Hare and the Tortoise

Hare loved to **brag** to the other animals about how fast he could run.

"I can move faster than anyone, yes, I can," he said. "Why, with one leg tied behind my back, I can still run faster than Zebra."

"And with both of my legs tied to my ears, I can out-hop Frog," he said. "No sirree, nobody can beat me!"

Whenever he started saying these things, Hare would **strut** around on his back legs and wiggle his little tail. **Needless** to say, his bragging and strutting did not make Hare popular with the other animals.

Most annoyed of all was **Tortoise**. She was a kind and **modest** creature, and Hare's **boasting** drove her crazy.

"You may be fast, but *even you* can be beaten," she told Hare during one of his more **obnoxious** "puff-a-thons." ("Puff-a-thon" was a word the other animals had invented to describe Hare's way of puffing himself up with **praise**.)

"Ha!" **chortled** Hare. "You think *you* can beat *me*?" (Of course, that wasn't exactly what Tortoise had said, but Hare was not a very good listener.)

Hare was so amused by the thought of Tortoise beating him in a race that he fell on the ground laughing. He laughed so hard that tears filled his eyes.

"Tortoise, you're so slow you couldn't beat me even if I were tied to a tree!" Hare **taunted**.

"Is that so?" said Tortoise, who was getting so mad that her shell was growing hot.

"Let's just have a race and we'll see," said Hare.

So they agreed on a **racecourse** and set the start and finish lines.

As they stood at the starting line, Beaver shouted, "Ready . . . set . . . go!"

Hare hopped quickly down the road and

disappeared from view while Tortoise **shuffled** along at her **plodding** pace.

After a few minutes, Hare looked over his shoulder and could not even see Tortoise behind him. "What am I rushing for?" he asked himself. "I've got plenty of time. And I never had my lunch."

He stepped off the road and went hunting for carrots and cabbages in a farmer's field. Finding a **plentiful** supply, he ate until his stomach hurt.

Hare wandered back to the road and still could not see Tortoise coming. Feeling pretty sleepy after his big lunch, he said to himself, "I think I'll take a quick nap."

Lying down on a soft patch of grass in the warm sun, Hare fell asleep.

When he woke up, he had no idea how much time had passed, but he had a feeling he had been napping a long time. "I'd better get moving," he said as he stood up and **stretched** his legs and ears.

That was when he heard shouting in the distance. He caught the words, "Come on! You can do it!"

Hare looked down the road, and what he saw gave him the shock of his life. There was Tortoise, just a few feet away from the finish line! Even worse, all the other animals were cheering for her!

Hare ran as fast as he could. He was **gasping** for breath, but he didn't slow down. Tortoise plopped over the finish line just seconds before Hare reached the spot.

Exhausted and **embarrassed**, Hare flopped down beside Tortoise. Tortoise smiled sweetly at him and said, "Sorry, Hare. Slow but **steady** wins the race."

VII. The Princess and the Pea

Once upon a time, there was a prince who wanted to marry a princess. But he wanted her to be a real princess, not a fake princess.

He traveled all over the world looking for one. During his travels he met dozens of young women who claimed to be princesses, but something about them always made him a little **suspicious**.

"I am a princess," said one young lady with a **haughty** air. She had hair that hung down to the floor. "I wash my hair six times a day and have ten servants whose only job it is to brush and comb my beautiful hair."

But when the young lady stepped on her own hair by accident, suddenly she was as bald as a baby—her long blond hair had been a wig!

Then there was another "princess" who, during dinner one evening, told the prince how important it is to have proper **etiquette**. "Good manners are a sign of **royalty**," she said.

At that moment, she grabbed a **fistful** of baked frog legs, gnawed on them with her mouth hanging open, then **belched** so loudly that all the people at the table dropped their forks.

The prince returned home sad and fearful that he might never find a real princess to marry.

One night there was a terrible storm, with thunder, **lightning**, and buckets of rain. It was scary!

Suddenly a knock was heard on the castle door. The king himself, dressed in his **pajamas** and a bathrobe, went to answer it since all the servants were asleep.

There stood a young woman who was quite a sight. She had water running down her hair and clothes and out the toes of her shoes. In a word, she was a mess.

"May I come in?" she asked. "I am a princess, and my **coach** broke down on the road."

The queen had followed her husband to the

door. She stared at the young woman and thought, "She doesn't look like a princess, but we'll find out soon enough."

The queen rushed to one of the castle's guest rooms and **stripped** away all the bedding. She put a single pea on the bed frame.

On top of the pea, the queen—huffing and puffing—piled twenty **mattresses**. Then she put another twenty **quilts** on top of the mattresses. The bed reached almost to the ceiling and the young lady had to climb a ladder to get into it.

The next morning, the storm was over and the sun was shining. The young woman took a bath and changed into clean, dry clothes. She came to the breakfast table looking quite lovely—except for her tired-looking eyes.

"How did you sleep, my dear?" asked the queen.

"I'm sorry to say I did not sleep a wink," said the young woman. "I felt like there was a huge rock in my bed, and I tossed and turned all night. Now I'm black and blue all over. It was awful."

The king, queen and prince clapped their hands with joy and hugged her, for they knew that only a *real* princess would be so **sensitive** and **tender-skinned** as to feel a tiny pea through twenty mattresses and twenty quilts.

The prince found that the princess was as kind and wise as she was sensitive. He fell in love with her and asked her to marry him, which she did.

As for the pea, it was put into a **museum** where you can still see it, unless someone has stolen it.

And that is a true story.

VIII. The Ugly Duckling

Once upon a time, there was a mother duck who lived on a river by an old farmhouse.

Mother Duck sat on her nest waiting for her eggs to **hatch**. She had been waiting a long time and was bored. But at last the eggs began to crack open one by one. "Peep! Peep! Peep!" said the baby ducks. "Quack, quack," said Mother Duck.

The baby ducks looked around. "How large the world is," they said. "There is so much more room here. Our shells were so small."

Mother Duck laughed and said, "If you think this is big, wait until you see the garden and the fields."

She stood and counted the baby ducks.

"One, two, three, four . . . ." Then she saw that one egg—the biggest one—had not yet hatched. With a sigh, Mother Duck sat down on the nest again.

At last the big egg hatched, and out popped a duckling that was large and gray and quite ugly.

Mother Duck wondered why this one wasn't little and yellow like her other babies. "Maybe it was a turkey egg I was sitting on," she said.

The next day she took all five ducklings to the water. In they jumped, one after another. They bobbed up and down with their legs **paddling** under them. She saw how well the ugly duckling swam and decided he could not be a turkey.

Then she took her babies to the farmyard. All of the ducks came to see them. One nasty duck flew over and bit the ugly duckling on his neck.

"Leave him alone!" cried Mother Duck. "He's not doing any harm."

"He is so big and funny-looking—he should not be **allowed** to live here with us," said the nasty duck.

"But he is very nice, and he swims well— even better than the others," said Mother Duck. "I think he will grow up to be quite strong," she said, **stroking** the ugly duckling's neck.

As the days went by, the poor ugly duckling was not treated well by the other ducks. They bit him, pushed him, and made fun of him. Even his own brothers and sisters were not nice to him. They said things like "I wish the cat would catch you and eat you."

One day he ran away, feeling certain that no one cared about him. He met some wild ducks by a **marsh**. "What kind of duck are you?" they asked. "You are very ugly, but that's OK as long as you don't try to marry anyone in our family."

The ugly duckling moved along to another marsh where two wild geese were **friendlier** to him. They warned him that there were **hunters** with guns nearby.

Pop! Pop! Gunshots sounded in the air. Then the duckling heard the barks of hunting dogs, and he was **terrified**. A big dog **sniffed** at him. The dog thrust his nose close to the duckling and showed his sharp teeth.

Then the dog **dashed** away through the water. *That was lucky!* thought the ugly duckling. *I'm so ugly that even a dog won't bite me.*

A storm **forced** the duckling to look for **shelter**. He found a poor little cottage and slipped inside. Living there were an old woman, a cat, and a hen.

The old woman could not see well and thought the ugly duckling must be a big, fat duck. "Lucky me," she said. "Perhaps it will lay some eggs." So she let him stay for three weeks to see if he would lay eggs—but, of course, he could not.

After a while, the duckling began to miss swimming. He told the hen.

"That's silly," she said.

"But it's so **delightful** to feel the water all around you when you dive to the bottom," he said.

"You must be crazy!" she snapped. "And you talk too much. You should try to lay some eggs or learn to purr like the cat."

"You don't understand me," said the duckling sadly. "I think I must go out into the world again."

"Yes, you do that," the hen said.

By now it was fall, and the leaves were turning yellow and brown. One evening at sunset, a flock of beautiful birds flew out of the bushes into the sky, heading south for the winter. They were white, with long, lovely necks and **glorious** wings. They were swans, but the duckling didn't know what they were called—he just knew he'd never seen anything so beautiful.

Winter came, and it grew colder. The duckling had to swim to keep the water in the marsh from **freezing**. But he grew tired and one night became frozen in the ice.

A farmer found him early the next morning. He broke the ice, carried the duckling home and warmed him.

The farmer's children wanted to play with him, but the duckling was terrified of them. He **fluttered** into the milk jug and spilled milk everywhere. The wife clapped her hands, and that frightened him even more. He flew into a large tub of butter and then into the **flour**. What a mess!

The wife **screamed** and tried to throw things at him, while the children laughed and tried to catch him. Luckily, the door was open and the duckling was able to escape into the snow.

The poor duckling lived through the hard, cold winter. Then spring came, and the sun warmed him. He stretched his wings—now much stronger than before—and flew up into the sky. Before he knew it, he found himself over a large garden full of **flowering** trees.

From behind some bushes floated three beautiful white swans, **gliding** lightly over the water. The duckling recalled the lovely birds, and he felt sad.

"If I approach these birds, they will just laugh at me and probably bite me for being so ugly," thought the duckling, as he landed in the water near the swans.

Ashamed of the way he looked, he hung his head. But what was that he saw in the clear water? His own **image**—no longer a **clumsy**, ugly, gray bird—but now a **graceful** and beautiful white swan!

Suddenly he felt glad that he had been through all those **sorrows** because now he would enjoy so much more all the happiness and good **fortune** in his **future**.

The three lovely swans swam around him, stroking his neck with their beaks as a welcome.

Some children came running into the garden and threw bread and cake into the water to feed the swans.

"See, there is a new one!" cried the smallest child. The others were **delighted** and ran to their father and mother, dancing, clapping their hands, and shouting, "Another swan has come—a new one has arrived!"

The children threw more food in the water. "The new one is the most beautiful of all," they said. "He is so young and handsome!" The older swans **bowed** their heads before him.

Then he felt quite shy and hid his head under his wing, for he didn't know what to do. He was so happy, but not full of pride. He had been hated and treated badly for his ugliness. Now he heard them say he was the most beautiful of all the birds!

The sun shone warm and bright. He fluffed his feathers, lifted his **slender** neck and cried with joy, "I never dreamed of such happiness as this when I was an ugly duckling!"

 IX. The Adventures of Tom Thumb

Once upon a time many years ago, a powerful old **wizard** named Merlin was tired and hungry from a long journey he was making. **Disguised** as a **beggar**, he stopped at the cottage of a poor farmer and his wife.

Right away they welcomed Merlin and invited him to share their meal. He was moved by their kindness. But while they ate, Merlin noticed that the couple seemed sad, and he asked them why.

"Ah," said the wife, with tears in her eyes, "We have no child. We'd love to have a son— even a little son no bigger than my husband's thumb. That would make us happy."

As Merlin left the cottage, he thought about

the woman's words. He was amused by the thought of a boy no bigger than a man's thumb. As soon as Merlin reached Fairyland, he asked his good friend the Fairy Queen if she could grant the woman's wish.

"I can and I will," she laughed.

So the farmer's wife soon had a son who—to everyone's surprise—was no bigger than his father's thumb. His parents loved him dearly and made a cradle for him from a walnut shell. They called him Tom Thumb.

One night the Fairy Queen flew in a window of the cottage, kissed the baby's cheek, and promised to help him should he ever need it.

Then she ordered her fairy tailors to make Tom a special suit of clothes. They made him a shirt from a spider's web, a jacket of **thistledown**, pants from apple rind and a tiny pair of mouse-skin shoes lined with fur. On his head, they put an oak-leaf cap. The next morning, his mother was very surprised to see him in his new clothes.

As Tom grew older—but no bigger—he was full of mischief and curiosity. With other boys in the village, he would play with cherry pits.

When Tom lost his, he would creep into the bags of other boys to steal their pits.

One boy caught Tom doing this and pulled the string of the bag tight, almost choking poor Tom. Then he shook the bag around, **bruising** Tom's little body. "Please let me out," begged Tom. The boy let him go, and Tom never stole anything again.

But he was always getting into trouble.

One day Tom's mother was making a batter pudding. When she left the kitchen for a moment, Tom climbed to the edge of the bowl to see the pudding. But his foot slipped, and he fell into the batter.

His mother returned but didn't see him. She tied the pudding in a cloth and put it in a pot to boil. Tom, stuck inside the pudding and starting to feel very hot, kicked and **struggled**. His mother, seeing the pudding jumping around in the pot, thought it must be **bewitched**, so she threw it out the window.

A **tinker** who was passing by picked it up and put it in his hat, planning to eat it for dinner. But Tom finally got the batter out of his mouth and began shouting.

This scared the tinker so much that he flung the pudding away and ran off as fast as he could. The pudding broke apart in the fall, and Tom was set free.

Covered with batter, he ran home to his mother. She gave him a bath, fed him a raisin, kissed him, and put him to bed.

Another time, Tom's mother took him with her when she went to milk their cow. Because it was windy, she tied her little son to a **thistle** for safety while she milked the cow. But the cow was hungry, and seeing Tom's tasty-looking oak-leaf hat, she took a mouthful of thistle—and Tom with it!

"Help! Mother, help me!" cried Tom.

"Where are you, dear?" called his mother.

"In the cow's mouth!" screamed Tom.

Thinking Tom would die, his mother began to weep. But he wiggled and yelled, and the cow— surprised by the fuss in her mouth—opened her jaws and let Tom drop out. His mother caught him in her apron and took him safely home.

After that, Tom's father decided to take Tom along with him when he **plowed** his field. He made Tom a tiny whip from a straw to drive the ox with. Tom felt very proud, cracking his little whip and helping his father.

But one day he fell off the ox into the deep tracks made by the plow. An eagle spotted Tom and, thinking the boy was a mouse, swooped down and picked him up in her claws. The eagle carried him to a giant's castle, which stood on a tall mountain overlooking the sea.

The eagle decided Tom was too wiggly and tough to feed to her babies, so she dropped him in the giant's garden.

When the giant found Tom, he popped him in his mouth like a piece of candy. But Tom kicked and scratched the giant's huge mouth so much that the giant spit the boy out into the sea.

In the sea, Tom was swallowed in one gulp by a big fish. Soon this fish was caught by a fisherman, who sent it to King Arthur as a present.

When a cook in the king's kitchen cut open the fish, out jumped Tom Thumb! The cook quickly showed him to the king.

King Arthur was so enchanted that he made Tom his court jester. Tom would do tricks, make funny speeches, and dance on people's hands. He was loved by all.

When the king went out riding on his horse, he often took Tom along. If it rained, Tom would creep into the king's pocket and take a nap.

One day King Arthur saw Tom looking sad and asked what was wrong. "Your Majesty," said Tom, "I'm truly happy here, but I miss my mother and father."

He told the king that his parents were poor country folk. The king said Tom must go see them and take them a present. He took Tom to his **treasury** and said, "Take all the money you can carry. Take it home to your parents."

But the only thing that Tom could carry—being still just as tiny as the day he was born—was one single silver coin. Even this was heavy on his back. And though Tom's parents lived quite near the castle, it took Tom two days and two nights to walk home, and he was exhausted when he got there.

His parents were thrilled to see him. They listened to his stories about life at the king's court and were very proud of their son.

After a few weeks at home, Tom decided to return to the king's court. It was wet and windy, and Tom's mother was afraid that if he walked back he'd be blown into a puddle and might drown. She waited until the wind was blowing toward King Arthur's castle. Then she tied Tom to a tiny umbrella and let the wind carry him.

But just as Tom **wafted** into the castle courtyard, the cook walked by carrying a large bowl of **porridge**, the king's favorite dish. Poor Tom fell into the bowl and splashed hot porridge in the cook's face.

The cook, a mean man, was very angry, and he told the king that Tom had spoiled the royal porridge on purpose.

Unfortunately, the king was in a very bad mood (because he hadn't had his porridge), and he sentenced Tom to be **beheaded**!

People in the castle, surprised by this harsh **punishment**, stood around with their mouths hanging open. Tom jumped into the nearest open mouth to hide. It belonged to the **miller**, who swallowed Tom.

The miller went home, but he began to feel sick, so he called his doctor. Tom began to dance and sing inside the miller, so when the doctor arrived, he thought the miller was bewitched. The doctor called in ten more doctors and twenty wise men.

As they stood around the miller's bed discussing what to do, the miller gave a huge burp and Tom shot out of his mouth.

The miller, in a fury, grabbed Tom and threw him out the window into a stream where, once again, he was swallowed by a fish.

The fish was caught and sold in the market to a **knight** who sent it to the queen as a present. She wanted it for dinner, so the cook cut open the fish. Once again Tom Thumb popped out!

The king, now in a good mood, was so happy to see Tom that he forgave him for **spoiling** the porridge.

In fact, the king ordered a new suit of clothes to be made for Tom. That was a good idea, since Tom's old clothes were very smelly after being in the batter pudding, the porridge, the cow's mouth, the giant's mouth, the miller's stomach, and—don't forget—the two fish bellies.

Tom's new shirt was made from a butterfly's wing, and his boots were of chicken skin. Instead of a horse, Tom was given a mouse to ride, and for a sword, he was given a golden needle.

One day the king and his knights were out hunting. Tom was riding his mouse next to them, when a big cat jumped off a wall and carried Tom and his mouse up a tree.

Tom drew his needle-sword and boldly poked the cat, which dropped them from its jaws. One of the knights caught Tom and the mouse as they fell from the tree and saved them both.

Soon after this, the Fairy Queen came to see Tom. She carried Tom away to Fairyland and kept him there for many years. By the time he returned, a different king ruled the country.

This new king did not know Tom and asked him many questions. Tom politely told his story, and the new king was **charmed** by him.

He liked Tom so much that he had a tiny golden chair made for him so that Tom could sit on the king's table while they ate. The king also ordered a beautiful golden palace to be built for Tom to live in. The palace was about twelve inches tall and had stables with six white mice that pulled a golden coach the size of a large peach.

Tom Thumb lived happily at the court for

many years, doing brave deeds and **entertaining** people with stories of his adventures. When he died, the king and his court were very sad. They put a lovely marble **monument** over his grave, and it's still there to this day.

GLOSSARY

Admitted	Charmed	Emperor
Adviser	Chortled	Empire
Allowed	Chow	Enchanted
Argued	Claws	Entertaining
Ashamed	Clumsy	Etiquette
Awaited	Coach	Exhausted
Beast	Cocky	Expected
Beggar	Courtiers	Exquisite
Begged	Cousins	Fangs
Beheaded	Creation	Fasten
Belched	Croak	Feed bin
Bewitched	Crooks	Fella
Blazed	Curious	Fistful
Boasted	Dashed	Flashed
Boasting	Delighted	Flour
Bothered	Delightful	Flowering
Bowed	Disappeared	Fluttered
Brag	Disappoint	Foiled
Bruising	Disguised	Forced
Canopy	Dough	Fortune
Cargo	Eluded	Fountains
Carriage	Embarrassed	Freezing

Friendlier	Knight	Pajamas
Frightened	Knock	Pantry
Future	Lickety-split	Peeling
Gasping	Licorice	Perked
Gingerbread	Lightning	Plentiful
Gliding	Looms	Plodding
Glorious	Magnificent	Plowed
Gnaw	Mantle	Porridge
Graceful	Marsh	Port
Growled	Matches	Praise
Guest	Mattresses	Pretended
Hare	Merchant	Proof
Harpsichord	Miller	Punishment
Hatch	Minister	Quaint
Haughty	Modest	Quilts
Heavyhearted	Monument	Racecourse
Host	Museum	Raisins
Howling	Needless	Royalty
Hunters	Obnoxious	Runaway
Ignored	Officials	Screamed
Image	One-quarter	Secretly
Invisible	Outfit	Sensitive
Jealous	Overjoyed	Servants
Kingdom	Paddling	Shelter

Shuffled	Tender-skinned
Sirree	Terrified
Slender	Thistle
Slimy	Thistledown
Sniffed	Three-quarters
Snug	Threshers
Sorrows	Threshing wheat
Spare	Tinker
Sparkles	Tortoise
Spoiling	Treasury
Squeaked	Unfortunately
Stable	Upsets
Statues	Vacation
Steady	Vain
Stretched	Vanity
Stripped	Wafted
Stroking	Whispered
Struggled	Whoa
Strut	Wizard
Suddenly	Yowled
Suspicious	
Taunt	
Taunted	
Teased	

Favorite Fairy Tales

Great job! You've finished reading the book. Now try these fun activities.

Word Whacker

Choose a word on the right that means the opposite of a word on the left. (Hint: Use the glossary to look up any meanings of the words on the left that you don't know.)

1. curious   modest
2. clumsy   graceful
3. ignored   ugly
4. vain   uninterested
5. exquisite   noticed

Story Puzzle

Who am I? This riddle gives clues to identify a fairy-tale character you just read about. First, think of what each line means. That will give you your clue. Then you can figure out whom the riddle is about. (Hint: Read pages 27-31.)

> I may not look like much at all,
> And in this skin, I'm not too tall.
> But once my true love I have found,
> Then on my head, I'll wear a crown.

Author Spotlight

Aesop was an ancient Greek storyteller. "The Tortoise and the Hare" is from his collection of animal tales, or fables. Each story has a hidden lesson or moral meant to improve how a person behaves.

Tales such as "Beauty and the Beast" were first written down by The Brothers Grimm. The original stories they collected were often cruel or sad. Once the tales became popular with young readers, the brothers made the fairy tales softer and sweeter.

As a child in Denmark, Hans Christian Andersen was teased because of his plain and awkward looks. One of his most famous stories is "The Ugly Duckling," which is based on his unhappy childhood.

LeapFrog Writer's Club

Choose a fairy-tale character you've read about. Try writing a riddle describing your character for your friends to solve.

Reading SERIES

Favorite Fairy Tales

Succeed in rea...... ...... step by step!

Favorite Fairy Tales

Peter Pan

The Secret Garden

Treasure Island

The Wind in the Willows

The Wizard of Oz

LeapFrog SchoolHouse™

A Division of LeapFrog Enterprises, Inc. Emeryville, CA 94608

US: (800) 883-7430

www.LeapFrogSchoolHouse.com

LEAPPAD is a registered trademarks of LeapFrog Enterprises, Inc.

LEAPFROG, SCHOOLHOUSE, QUANTUM PAD, the GO sound and the CHECKERBOARD PATTERN are trademarks of LeapFrog Enterprises, Inc.

© 1999 LeapFrog Enterprises, Inc. All rights reserved.

BOOK PRINTED IN CHINA

ISBN 1-58605-918-1

9 781586 059187

BP600-02066